A BIRD'S EYE VIEW
ATTICUS
SEES
San Francisco

WRITTEN BY: DEMI FRANDSEN

ILLUSTRATED BY: IY CAPENER

Acknowledgements:

I'd like to thank the little bird that made her nest on the top
of our favorite pizza place. This bird started my son's
and my conversation of where we would live and travel
if we were birds. It was that conversation that inspired
The Bird's Eye View book series.

I'd also like to thank my 4th grade teacher, Mrs. Wolf,
for inspiring me to dream big. She told me, "The world is yours,"
and I found genuine power in that phrase.
I owe a very enthusiastic thanks to my amazing husband
for supporting me and encouraging me to
take a risk and follow a dream.

I want to thank my sister, Brittney, for dedicating time
and lending her talent to help design this book series.

I also want to thank Abby Frandsen for editing photographs
used to create this book.

Caroline, thank you for helping me polish the words to
tell Atti's story in the best way possible.

Irelynd, thank you for making Atticus come to life through
your brilliant artwork and creative mind!

For Sawyer, Leo, and Scout. The world is yours, my little birdies.

Somewhere in a tree in a town in the Midwest,
live a mama finch and a baby finch in a cozy little nest.

The baby Finch is Atticus,
and he loves to explore,
to see the world, to meet new friends,
to open every door.

Mama Finch has seen the world
from her bird's eye view.
She saw wondrous places
and wants Atti to see them, too.

She sends him on adventures
to explore from east to west.
At night he flies back home
to Mama waiting in their nest.

Today's adventure is waiting; Atticus is ready to take flight.
"San Francisco, here I come!" and he flaps with all his might!

His wings start moving up and down as little Atti soars.
Mama Finch hollers out, "Remember, the world is yours!"

Mama Finch told Atti to start flying to the west,
The coast of California is a long way from the nest!

San Francisco is an exciting city nestled on the bay,
Atti heads to the Pacific Ocean, happily on his way.

He watches for the coastline
as he flies westward through the sky.
He sees the ocean stretching out
and buildings reaching high!

It's San Francisco! There it is!
He claps his wings with pure delight.
He heads to the Golden Gate Bridge,
his first San Francisco site!

The brightly colored bridge
is nearly two miles long.
Steel cables run between concrete blocks,
which makes it very strong.

The concrete blocks are anchored
deep down to the ocean floor.
Its suspended roadway stretches out,
connecting shore to shore.

Around 112,000 vehicles
cross the bridge every day.
What an exciting way to travel
across the San Francisco Bay!

Atticus races cars on the
bridge down below.
He travels up the coastline
looking for some place to go.

Fisherman's Wharf is a popular spot
with so many things to see!
There are fishing boats docked in the marina
and ferries out to sea.

He spots a wartime submarine
and some historic battleships.
He sees restaurants selling seafood.
He wants some fish and chips!

Flying near the water,
Atti spots Pier 39.
It's home to many attractions
and festive by design.

Street performers perform
music and art on the street.
There is a dock covered in sea lions
that Atti wants to meet!

"K Dock" was once only for boats,
but after an earthquake - things changed.
Sea Lions moved in and liked it there.
Now things have rearranged.

These barking friends feel safe right here -
there's plenty of food and sun.
They spend their days lounging on the docks,
which is fun for everyone!

Atti flies toward the dock
and sees a friendly pup.
He says, "Hi! I'm Atticus."
The baby sea lion looks up.

"Hello, Atticus! My name is Felix.
It is such a pleasure to meet you!
I've never seen you here before.
Are you just flying through?"

"I'm here on an adventure!
Mama sent me to explore."
"I love exploring!" cries Felix,
"in the ocean and on shore!"

"What is that?" Atti asks
as he points out to sea.
"That's Alcatraz Island," Felix says,
"come on, follow me!"

Felix dives into the water
and leads Atti from below.
They journey towards the island,
both smiling as they go!

"Alcatraz is an old prison
on an island off the shore.
It was also used as a military fortress
during the Civil War."

Atticus is fascinated
with the island and its fame.
Felix said that people call it
"The Rock" as a nickname.

Swimming back to his dock,
Felix waves his fin goodbye.
"Enjoy San Francisco!"
he says to Atticus in the sky.

The city is full of color!
Houses are painted in every shade.
A row of houses called The Painted Ladies
stand in a rainbow parade!

San Francisco is enchanting:
the colors, the buildings, and the coast!
Atti can't decide what part
of San Francisco he likes the most!

He sees a trolley driving by;
he wants to take a ride!
He finds a spot to sit
and looks out as it starts to glide.

Trolleys are called cable cars
because they're pulled from down below
From a cable under the street
that pulls them where they need to go.

San Francisco is the first city
to use this type of transportation.
It's a trademark for the city,
a traveling landmark for the nation!

When the trolley comes to one of its stops,
Atti gets off and waves goodbye.
"What a fun way to travel!
But now I think I'll fly!"

As he flies over the streets,
he sees one that curves and twists and bends.
From up above it looks like
a slithering snake that never ends!

Lombard Street has eight curvy turns
in one short little block,
It attracts many visitors
who have come for a winding walk.

He flies toward a part of town
that Mama told him to see.
"Chinatown will make you feel
like you're in a different country!"

Hundreds of red lanterns
are strung above the busy street.
The entrance is guarded by statues,
protecting those they greet.

Chinatown is massive!
It spreads 24 blocks wide.
Stores and streets full of Chinese culture
are bustling inside.

He admires every building
built in traditional Chinese style.
He samples delicious foods
while observing people for a while.

After taking in Chinatown
and all its festive fun,
Atticus flies to one last stop
before his trip is done.

The weather is just right
to catch a Giant's baseball game,
"Welcome to Oracle Park!"
he hears the announcer exclaim.

"Let's go Giants!"
the crowd chants from their seats.
He grabs his glove and hits the field
to join the other athletes.

This ballpark is phenomenal
with so much to see and do!
Sitting in the bleachers,
you can watch the game with an ocean view.

McCovey's Cove is part of the ocean
where fans can watch and float-
They race to balls hit into the water,
watching the whole game from their boat!

There is a hidden playground
where kids can run and slide,
The giant Coca Cola bottle
has four fun slides inside!

The 80-foot Coke bottle
isn't just for fun,
It also lights up each time
the Giants hit a homerun!

The stadium lights shine on the field
as the sky starts turning dark.
Atti knows it's time to wave goodbye
to the magical Oracle Park.

The sun starts setting on the bay,
and the stadium lights glow bright.
Atticus waves to San Francisco
as he starts flying through the night.

He journeys eastward through the night,
until he sees their nest.
Atticus had an exciting day,
but now he is ready to rest.

Mama Finch is waiting. He sees her spread her wings.
"Welcome home from your grand adventure!" Mama Finch sings.

He tells about his glorious trip and all that he did see.
Atticus loved San Francisco, but he's glad to be home in his tree.

"It's time for sleep, my little bird," Mama Finch says with a grin.
"For when you wake up in the morning,
another adventure will begin!"

Take Atticus on your next adventure!
Have a parent help you cut out these Atticus figures,
paste them to a popsicle stick,
and take pictures of him on your own daily adventures!
Remember to tag him in your pictures and follow him on Instagram!

@atticusseestheworld
#attiadventures

Meet the Author

Demi Frandsen was born and raised in Idaho Falls, Idaho.
She graduated with her degree in Elementary Education from
Utah State University and taught for three years.
She is a mother to three outrageously lovely children
and wife to a wildly handsome man named Jeff.
She enjoys art, reading, running and sports.
Demi likes to spend her time adventuring and creating art
with her children. She believes there should be no such thing
as an ordinary day. Every day is a chance to explore, pretend,
create, and love.

Meet the Illustrator

Iy Capener is a doodler, reader, dancer, and
cinnamon-toast-enthusiast. She was born and raised in
Salt Lake Valley, Utah. As a young child, she constantly got
into trouble with her teachers for doodling all over her assignments.
As an older college student, her professors are less vocal,
but are still most likely tired of seeing a small bird peeking
through every assignment title and flying in and out of every
algebra equation. Iy now attends college in Provo with her
best friend and husband, Dane. Iy's dream is to draw everything,
but for now, she will settle for most things. (She also had a dream that
a zombie made of donuts was chasing her one time,
but that is a different type of dream entirely.)

Gabe & Adele,

I hope you enjoy your adventures with Atticus! We miss you guys!

♡ Demi Frandsen

Made in the USA
Lexington, KY
01 November 2019